For all inquiries, please contact us at:
info@puppysmiles.org

To see more of our books, visit us at:
www.PuppyDogsAndIceCream.com

Alphabet of Friends

A is for Amber

B is for Becky

C is for Chris

D is for David

E is for Ellen

F is for Fran

G is for Garret

H is for Hailey

I is for Irene

J is for Jason

K is for Kristine

L is for Luke

M is for Michael

N is for Nicole

O is for Owen

P is for Penelope

Q is for Quinn

R is for Ricky

S is for Steve

T is for Tammie

U is for Ursula

V is for Victoria

W is for Winnie

X is for Xavier

Y is for Yazmin

Z is for Zack

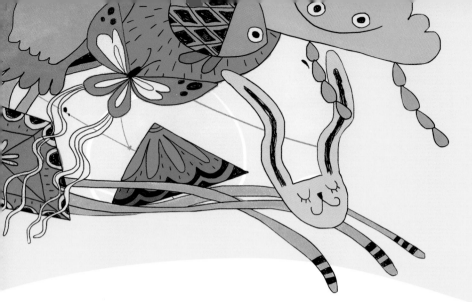

This is a story...
　　about little Sarah Glee,

and her twenty six friends...
　　with names from A to Z.

So get on-board...
　　this silly alphabet ride,

as your new alphabet friends...
　　teach you to be happy inside.

From Amber to Zack...
    don't forget Ellen and Steve,

they'll be your friends too...
    whenever you need.

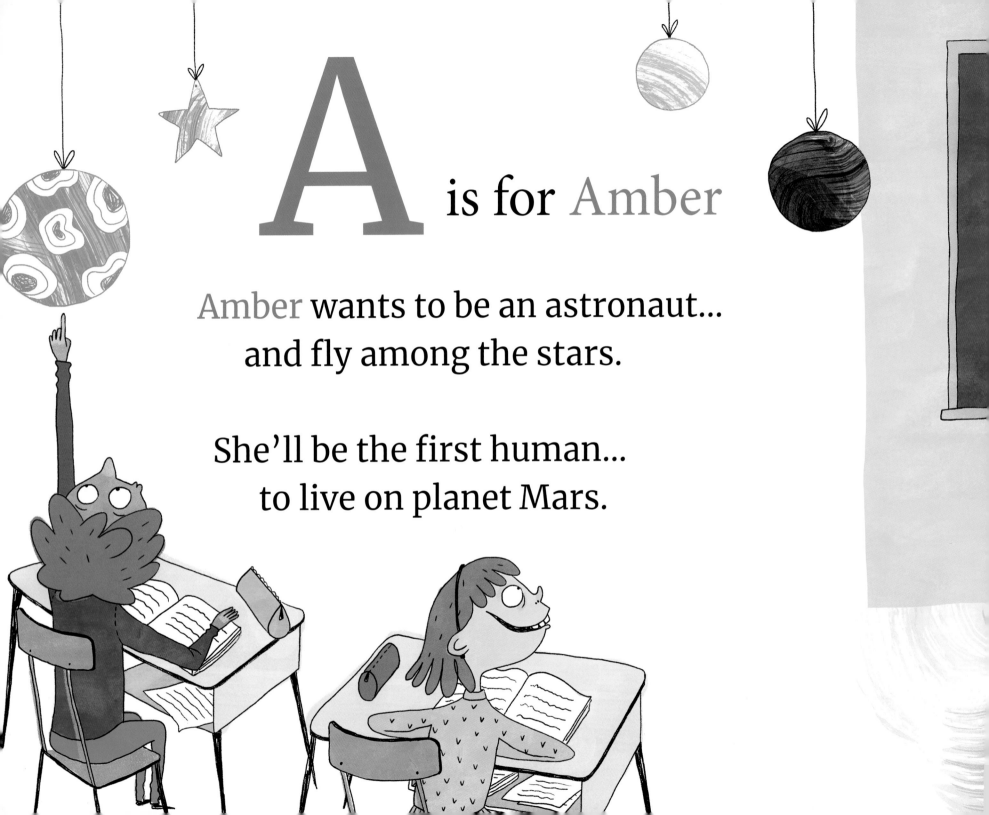

A is for Amber

Amber wants to be an astronaut...
and fly among the stars.

She'll be the first human...
to live on planet Mars.

B is for Becky

Becky's cat "Tiger"...
is now stuck up in a tree,

After chasing chubby squirrels...
like every cat in history.

C is for Chris

Chris recites his lines...
    bent down on one knee,

Looking back at the world's...
    only whistling tree.

D is for David

David screams...
   a halloween "***Booooo!***"

Still scary after stepping...
   in stinky dog doooo.

E is for Ellen

Ellen's friends know her...
as a master baker.

One day she'll be famous...
as a great cookie maker.

F is for Fran

Fran jumped on the table...
getting food all over the place.

Pizzas fly high in the sky...
while Fred gets a pie in the face.

G is for Garret

Dreaded Pirate Garret...
  looks out for the weekend.

So much cake on the horizon...
  so many birthdays to attend.

H is for Hailey

Hailey loves to get hugs...
as all little girls do,

But she also knows...
that moms need hugs too.

I is for Irene

Irene stands up...
  to give a mighty speech,

Inspiring others...
  to help clean up the beach.

J is for Jason

Jason holds his breath...
 diving deep into the ocean,

Swimming with whales...
 copying their big-tail motion.

K is for Kristine

Kristine's froggy umbrella...
blocks rain from the sky,

Helping her little brother...
make it to school nice and dry.

L is for Luke

Luke shouts, **"Ahhhhhh"**
at the top of his lungs,

As the roller-coaster rattles...
across the rickety rungs.

M is for Michael

Michael splashes bubbles...
high into the air.

His birds don't do dishes...
but Michael doesn't care.

N is for Nicole

Nicole wants to be...
a world-famous actress.

Just don't tell her she needs...
100 years of practice.

O is for Owen

Owen winds up...
    for a speeding curve-ball.

The umpire yells *Strike!*
    It's the game's winning call.

P is for Penelope

Penelope pretends...
to be a magical unicorn,

Or maybe she's a big, pink pony...
with one big, long horn.

Q is for Quinn

Quinn forgets about school...
floating in a warm bubble-bath.

Doesn't care about homework...
not history or math.

R is for Ricky

Ricky holds the door open...
    and gets a pinch on the cheek.

He smiles politely,
    "hi Grandma... you *antique*."

S is for Steve

Steve is a "man's man,"
   who camps and sleeps among rocks.

When he hikes without shoes on...
   he ends up with dirty socks.

T is for Tammie

Tammie is a tomboy...
    and collects jumping frogs,

It's her parents' own fault...
    they said "No more dogs."

U
is for Ursula

Ursula's long leopard legs...
    make her really fast,

Little Penny is now...
    the best hand-raiser in class.

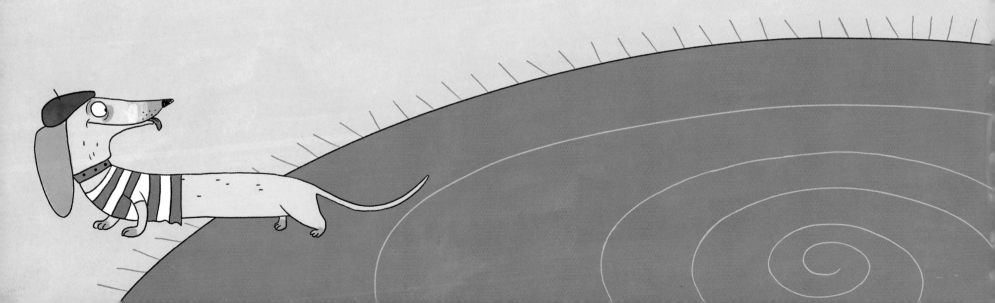

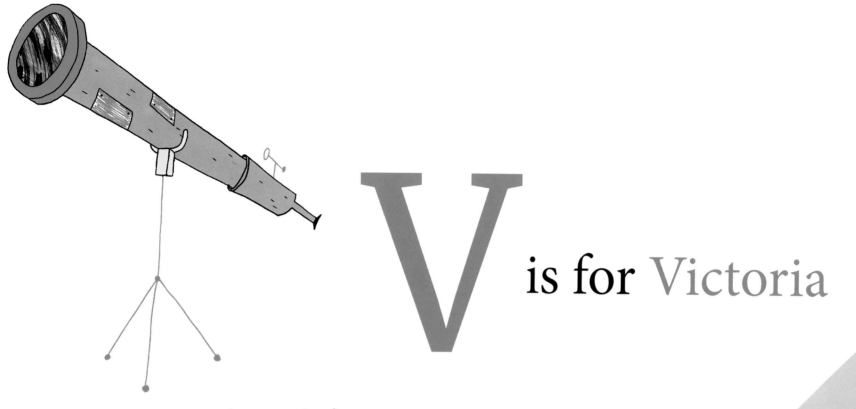

V is for Victoria

Victoria's vision board...
shows a plan for her life.

She'll be a world-famous scientist...
a mom and a wife.

W is for Winnie

Winnie's hair whips whimsically...
in the winter wind briskly.

While Winnie's dog Willie...
wags his wiggly tail wildly.

X is for Xavier

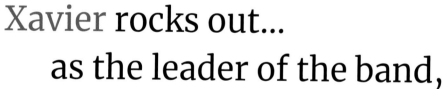

Xavier rocks out...
    as the leader of the band,

The bang of the drums...
    louder than a yellow cat can stand.

Y is for Yazmin

Yazmin and her friends...
share an elephant ride,

Gliding down a purple trunk...
a.k.a., an "elephant slide."

Z is for Zack

Zack ZZZZ's like a zombie...
he doesn't have school today.

It's Saturday after all...
It's gonna be a great day!

Your future is made of wishes...
sometimes hopes and then dreams.

Life isn't so bad...
it's not as hard as it seems.